D0057511

Meghan Rose
Knows It All

written by
Lori Z. Scott

illustrated by
Stacy Curtis

Standard®
PUBLISHING

Cincinnati, Ohio

Published by Standard Publishing, Cincinnati, Ohio
www.standardpub.com

Text Copyright © 2010 by Lori Z. Scott
Illustrations Copyright © 2010 by Stacy Curtis

All rights reserved. #25446. Manufactured in Grand Rapids,
MI, USA, August 2011. No part of this book may be
reproduced in any form, except for brief quotations in reviews,
without the written permission of the publisher.

Printed in: United States of America
Project editor: Diane Stortz

Scripture taken from the *HOLY BIBLE, NEW
INTERNATIONAL VERSION®. NIV®*. Copyright © 1973,
1978, 1984 by Biblica, Inc.™ Used by permission of
Zondervan. All rights reserved.

ISBN 978-0-7847-2931-1

Library of Congress Cataloging-in-Publication Data

Scott, Lori Z., 1965-
  Meghan Rose knows it all / written by Lori Z. Scott ;
illustrated by Stacy Curtis.
       p. cm.
  Summary: First-grader Meghan Rose, caught up in a contest
with Sophie to prove who is smarter, does not see that her
friend Lynette is upset, but before long she has learned the
difference between "smart" and "wise." Includes discussion
questions and activities.
  ISBN 978-0-7847-2931-1 (perfect bound)
  [1. Contests--Fiction. 2. Wisdom--Fiction. 3. Pride and vanity-
-Fiction. 4. Schools--Fiction. 5. Christian life--Fiction.] I.
Curtis, Stacy, ill. II. Title.
  PZ7.S42675Mdk 2010
  [Fic]--dc22
                                    2010029317

16 15 14 13 12 11   2 3 4 5 6 7 8 9 10

Contents

1

The Challenge

"I think that weird Monday morning spelling pretest has to mean something," I said to my friends Lynette and Kayla.

We sat down to eat lunch. "Knowing Mrs. Arnold, you're probably right," Lynette said. "Let's see . . . she gave us *gem*, *sand*, and *stone*."

"Don't forget *mud* and *dirt* too," Kayla said. She ripped open her chip bag and stuffed corn chips into her mouth. "I love those words. But not as much as I love the word *duck*."

Chip chunks flew out of her mouth as she talked. One hit Lynette *SPLAT* in the face.

Glaring, Lynette wiped off her cheek. "Swallow."

Kayla swallowed. Twice. It seemed to help.

"I think it means we'll study Egypt," Lynette said. "All the words fit." She straightened her big puffy hair bow. "I checked out a library book about Egypt. The Egyptians used gems in their jewelry and carved statues out of stone. They used mud to make bricks. Plus there's a lot of sand in Egypt."

"The words also fit if we study rocks," I said. "I know tons of stuff about rocks. That's because my grandpa collects them.

He calls me his rock hound."

"I had a pet rock hound once," Kayla said. "It was hard to train."

Lynette and I stared at her. "You mean a pet rock," I said slowly.

"That too," Kayla said. "It was still hard to train. Whenever I took my rock for a walk, it just dragged along the ground. When I tried to teach it how to fetch, it just sat there. I had to fetch my own sticks."

"Too bad," I said.

"I know," Kayla said. She started counting on her fingers. "My rock also couldn't speak, beg, come, dance, or shake. But with a lot of hard work, I taught it how to sit and play dead."

"Wowie," I said, shaking my head. "Did you name it Rocky? Or Pebbles?"

"Don't be silly!" Kayla said. "I named it

Duck."

That's when I heard a snooty voice behind me say, "Who names a rock *Duck*?"

The voice belonged to Sophie. She's in first grade too, in Mrs. Killeen's class, right across the hall from our room.

Sophie stood there with her arms folded and her lips in a long flat line. Her eyes looked like hard brown marbles. She was wearing her hair in a French braid tied with a red ribbon that matched the ruffles on her shirt. Her jeans had jewels on them.

"Duck is a nice name," I said.

"Of course you'd like it, Meghan Rose," Sophie sneered. "You're not smart like me."

I frowned at her. "What does being smart have to do with ducks?"

"Nothing," Lynette said quickly. "She's

4

still mad at you for what happened during the Penny War."

Sophie ignored us. "I'll prove I'm the smartest. We'll have a contest. At recess."

"No thank you," I said.

"Are you afraid I'm right that I'm smarter?" Sophie asked. "Or are you too chicken to find out?"

Kayla looked up and down at me. "Well, she might be a chicken, but she's definitely not a duck. Now, I look a LOT like a duck. Yellowish hair. Cute piggy tails. Not that ducks have piggy tails, but piggy tails are more duckish than piggish, don't you think?"

"Kayla, you're not helping," I said.

"Well?" Sophie said.

Sitting up stiff and tall, I turned my back on her. I took a huge bite of my sandwich so

5

I wouldn't have to talk. Because whenever I talked to Sophie, my mouth always seemed to get me in trouble.

"Tomorrow. Lunch recess. Meet by the monkey bars," Sophie said.

I heard her walk away. I kept chewing.

"A panther," Kayla said. "I'm a duck, and Sophie's a panther. Or something black and scary with big teeth. Like a comb." She elbowed me. "But Sophie's wrong about you. After all, you can't be a chicken if you're a rock hound."

Lynette patted my shoulder. "Never mind," she said. "Just swallow."

I did. Twice. It didn't help.

2

Meghan Rocks!

After lunch, Mrs. Arnold gave everyone a sock tied shut at the top. "Without looking, feel your sock and guess what might be in it."

Mine felt heavy, hard, and lumpy. Like a rock. I raised my hand.

So did a lot of other kids.

"Kayla?" Mrs. Arnold said.

"It's a dried-up marshmallow," Kayla said.

"Interesting idea," Mrs. Arnold said. I waved my hand in the air. "Ryan?"

"Bubblegum. It gets hard if it sits out too long."

Mrs. Arnold smiled. "It does. Any other ideas?"

Stretching my arm higher, I bounced in my seat. Mrs. Arnold said, "Abigail."

"I think it's a monkey brain."

"Could be," Mrs. Arnold said. I made brainless monkey sounds, *ooh-ooh-ooh*. Mrs. Arnold called on Adam.

"I think it's a yo-yo," he said.

My heart went *BUMP-bump*. So did my mouth. "IT'S A ROCK!" I blurted.

"No it's not," Lynette said, with a prim look. "It's probably a small statue from Egypt. Because we're going to study Egypt. Right, Mrs. Arnold?"

"Actually," Mrs. Arnold said, "Meghan is right. Open up your socks and take a look."

All the kids dumped out their socks. Mrs. Arnold walked around the room.

"We're starting a new unit on rocks. If you glance around, you'll see that rocks come in many shapes and sizes." She held up Kayla's rock. "Some feel light, like a sponge."

"Or a marshmallow!" Kayla said.

I raised my hand. "That rock is called pumice. It's an igneous rock."

Mrs. Arnold nodded. "Very good, Meghan. Can you explain what *igneous* means?"

"My grandpa told me igneous rocks are sometimes called fire rocks because they come from volcanoes. He says pumice has a bunch of holes in it because when the lava cools off, all the gas bubbles pop."

"Gas pops—*burp*—from me when I drink soda," Ryan said. "Or if I eat my mom's chili. The thing is, you can burp anywhere, and that's OK. But you'd better be in a big room if it's the other kind of gas popping out. And even then, it's a good idea to blame it on your cat."

"Wowie," Kayla said. "I've never heard a rock burp before!"

"Pumice doesn't burp," I said. "But all those holes make it light. It even floats."

I heard whispering around the room. This rock fact seemed to WOW a lot of kids. Either that or they finally figured out what kind of gas Ryan was talking about.

"What about my rock?" Lynette asked, holding it up. "It has stripes."

I looked at Mrs. Arnold. She nodded.

"It's a *gneiss* rock," I said.

"I know it's nice," Lynette said, "but what is it called?"

"It's called gneiss," I said. "Its name sounds like the word *nice*, but it's spelled *G-N-E-I-S-S*."

Another whisper went through the class. Kids looked at me with wide eyes. This was fun. I pointed at Abigail's rock.

"That one's called a geode," I said. "It looks ho-hum, monkey-brain plain on the outside, but the inside is filled with sparkly crystals. Except there's no way of knowing about all that WOWIE inside until you open it up."

Mrs. Arnold smiled. "Class, it looks like we have a rock expert with us. Meghan, you can be my special helper during this unit."

Every eye turned my way. The words "special helper" hung in the air like the ring of a bell.

I felt a little smart. More than a little smart — smarty-smart.

Smarter than Kayla, who couldn't tell the difference between a rock and a marshmallow.

Smarter than Adam, who only thought about yo-yos.

Smarter than Ryan, who called burping a sport.

Smarter than Lynette, whose puffy hair bow made her brain seem larger than it really is.

I felt Einstein smart.

Einstein was a smarty-smart scientist who lived a long time ago. He knew lots of stuff about lots of stuff.

Except I don't believe Einstein knew how to use a hairbrush. In all his pictures, his white hair sticks out like he got hit with a bolt of lightning.

Grandpa told me Einstein once said, "I am enough of an artist to draw freely on my imagination." And I know what he meant!

That's because I not only draw freely on my imagination, I also draw freely on my mom's calendar, the back covers of my favorite books, my arm (but only if I have smelly markers), and the sides of my math worksheets.

Mrs. Arnold continued the lesson, and I used my smarty-smart brain to think about Sophie's challenge.

I drew freely on my imagination . . . and I liked the picture I made. Me. By the monkey bars. With my smarty-smart brain. Thinking smarty-smart things. About smarty-start stuff. Acting so smarty-smart that even Sophie had to agree that I was smarty-smarter than her.

That's why I decided to meet Sophie the next day at recess and accept her challenge after all.

3

Your Highness

"You're really going to meet Sophie after lunch?" Ryan asked me the next morning.

The bus hit a bump, and I bounced in my seat. There should be a rule against bouncy buses, but apparently there is not.

I shifted my backpack to the floor. "Sure. Why not?"

Ryan shrugged. "Oh, I don't know. Maybe the fact that Sophie will do anything to win. And she's as mean as a panther."

"But she's not smarter than me," I said.

"Let's test your smarts then," Ryan said. "I found some jokes to share with Mrs. Arnold. They're perfect for this new unit. See if you can guess them."

"Let's do it," I said.

"What did Bugs Bunny say to the mountain?"

"Easy," I said. "What's up, Rock?"

"What's a rock's favorite food and favorite music?"

"Double easy. Rock candy. And rock and roll."

"Wowie," Ryan said. "You really are smart. But here's the toughest one. What do you call a scary sea creature that hardens into stone?"

I pretended to be stumped, but I knew the answer. I didn't tell Ryan, but Grandpa had

16

already told me these rock jokes last time we went rock hunting. But no sense taking away all the drama. "Could it be a . . . no, maybe a . . . wait, a—"

Ryan looked triumphant. "Give up?"

"I know! The Rock-ness Monster. Like the Loch Ness Monster."

Ryan's mouth fell open so wide I could have stuck my whole hand inside. He snapped it shut again. "Can I go with you at lunch recess and watch?" he said.

"Only if you treat me like a queen."

Grinning, Ryan bowed his head. "Your Highness."

On our way to our classroom, Ryan and I passed Robby, the kindergartener we'd met during the Penny War. He was down on one knee, struggling to tie his shoe.

"Hi, Robby," I said. "What's wrong?"

"It's my shoelaces," Robby said. He sniffled. "I keep tripping over them. And now they came untied again and—and I don't know how to tie shoes."

I knelt down next to him. "There's a trick to it. Want me to show you?"

Robby nodded. I showed him how to make a tree with one lace and then go around the tree and through the hole with the other. "Just like that," I said, pulling the laces tight.

"You're smart," Robby said. "Thanks!"

My chest seemed to swell like a balloon. I stood up and marched down the hall with my head held high. First Ryan realized how smart I was, and now Robby did too.

Before the morning announcements, I walked through the rows of desks spreading even more of my smartness around. "Try

18

twisting the lid the other way," I told Levi, who was having trouble opening his water bottle.

"It worked!" Levi said. "Thanks."

"Sharpen the other end of your pencil," I told Kayla. "That end is the eraser."

Kayla smacked her forehead. "Oops. I forgot."

I saw Adam fishing through his backpack. "If I were looking for math homework, I'd check in my spelling folder," I said.

Adam did. He found it. "How did you know?" he gasped. I tapped my forehead and smiled.

Abigail rushed over with a rock. "I found this in my driveway. Do you know what it is?"

Like a magician swooping aside his cape, I took the rock from her. I licked my

19

thumb and ran it over the surface. It made a slobbery streak. My grandpa always does that when he finds a rock. He says it brings out the color.

Plus it seemed to impress Abigail. She leaned closer. I held the stone up to the light. Lynette came over to watch.

"This is granite," I finally announced.

"Oh! Just like our bonus spelling word," Abigail said.

I nodded. "Which, by the way, I spelled correctly on the pretest."

"You're smart," Abigail said. "Hey, everyone! Meghan Rose knows it all."

"Yay!" Kayla yelled. She bounded over.

"What does she know?"

"More than Sophie," Ryan said, coming up beside me. "She's going to meet Sophie at lunch recess today and prove she's smarter. Right, Your Highness?"

I lifted my chin. "Right!"

Kids crowded around me, *oohing* and *ahhing*. But Lynette stayed back. Her face got red and her hands curled into little fists.

I'm smart enough to know when a good friend is angry.

But right then, I wasn't smart enough to care.

4
Rock the Boat

After lunch, I marched out to the playground like a queen, with kids from my class following me. Sophie was waiting, hands on her hips. Kids from Mrs. Killeen's class stood around her.

"Where's Lynette?" I whispered to Kayla.

"Jumping rope. Do you want to jump rope too?"

Before I could answer, Sophie said, "You

showed up. That wasn't very . . . *smart*."

"An insult," I said. "Ow, that . . . *smarts*."

Sophie made a huffing sound.

Kayla said, "Yay! Meghan wins. Let's go play jump rope now."

"She didn't win anything. We haven't even started yet," Sophie said. She folded her arms. "I can spell the word *ridiculous*. Can you beat that?"

My friends gasped. I held my breath and thought hard. My hands started sweating. I rubbed them on my shirt while trying to work out the spelling for *ridiculous* in my head.

My effort was ridiculous. And this would be a ridiculous way to lose. And I would lose ridiculously unless I struck back in some ridiculous way.

"Well? Can you spell it?" Sophie asked.

"Sure," I said quickly. "I-T."

She glared at me. "Nice try. I meant spell the word *ridiculous*."

Looking at my feet, I shook my head.

"Ha!" Sophie cried. "That proves I'm smarter than you!"

"Not yet," I said. "I can spell the words *metamorphic, sedimentary,* and *igneous*. All types of rocks. Can you beat that?"

Sophie ground her teeth. Finally she spat out, "No."

Kayla clapped, "Yay! It's a tie. Let's go play jump rope now."

"Wait," Ryan said. "You can't end with a tie."

"Yeah," said Abigail. "And Meghan Rose knows it all. Prove it, Meghan."

I licked my lips. My stomach fluttered.

Could I prove it? Maybe. "Have you ever played Concentration?" I asked.

Sophie hesitated. "Yes," she said slowly. "You slap your legs, then clap your hands, then snap your fingers to a beat. One person picks a topic. Then you take turns naming things in the topic until someone misses a beat or can't come up with an answer."

"So sit down and let's play it," I said. "We'll play three rounds. Whoever wins twice wins the game. Our friends can pick the topics."

Biting her lip, Sophie looked back at her friends. Then she nodded. "But my friend Carly picks the first topic."

"Deal," I said.

We sat. We got a beat going. *SLAP, CLAP, snap, snap, SLAP, CLAP, snap, snap.* Then we chanted,

"Let's play a game
of Concentration.
No mistakes or hesitation.
Speaking of—"
Snap, snap.
"Names of—"
Snap, snap."
"Animals!" Carly shouted.
Then we went back and forth, going
faster and faster.
"Chicken," I said.
"Snake."
"Donkey."
"Shark."
"Monkey."
"Lizard."
"Lion."
"Tiger."
"Hippo."

"Hamster."

"Turtle."

"Doggie."

"Giraffe."

"Bunny."

"Sheepdog."

"Wait!" Carly yelled. "Sophie already said doggie, so Meghan can't say sheepdog. Sophie wins the first round."

"I can't believe you didn't say DUCK!" Kayla yelled.

"Sorry," I said. "I should have said duck."

"Why do people always leave out the ducks?" Kayla wailed.

Sophie smirked. "Your turn."

"Right," I said. "Ryan can pick the next topic."

"Pick *ducks*," Kayla whispered loudly.

"That's not a topic," Ryan whispered loudly back.

I sighed.

We got the beat going. We chanted,

"Let's play a game

of Concentration.

No mistakes or hesitation.

Speaking of—"

Snap, snap.

"Names of—"

Snap, snap."

"Sports!" Ryan shouted.

We went back and forth again, faster and faster.

"Dance," said Sophie.

"Softball."

"Soccer."

"Basketball."

"Baseball."

"Hockey."

"Football."

"Gymnastics."

"Tennis."

"Swimming."

"Track."

"Volleyball."

"Checkers."

"Checkers isn't a sport!" Ryan cried. "Meghan wins round two."

A shot of WHOO-HOO pumped through my body. My hands tingled and my heart went *BUMP-bump*.

Kayla shook my arm. "Yay! It's a tie."

Sophie said. "NO! There's one round left."

"No, there's not," Kayla said. "The bell just rang. Recess is over. You constipated so hard, you didn't hear it."

"Concentrated," I said. "You mean we *concentrated*."

"That too," Kayla said.

"Fine," Sophie said. "We'll settle this tomorrow with a different test."

"Good," I said. "This was kind of fun, don't you think?"

"Winning is fun," Sophie said.

"So is playing," I said.

Sophie gave me a little push. "Get this straight. We weren't playing. And this isn't a game. And this isn't fun."

Kayla put her arm around me. She frowned at Sophie. "Pushing isn't nice. And this wasn't fun because everyone left out the ducks. Next time, put in a few ducks. Come on, Meghan. Let's go."

As we walked away, I searched the playground for Lynette. I spotted her in

31

line, waiting to go in. Looking sad. Why hadn't she come with Kayla and Ryan to cheer me on today?

I almost called out to her when Adam slapped me on the back. "Way to go, Meghan!"

"You're the smartest. I know it," said Abigail. She shouted, "Yay! Meghan, Meghan, Meghan!"

The cheering made me step tall like a queen. Or a show horse. Or Einstein, but without the crazy hair.

Lynette never glanced my way.

Froo Froo

On Wednesday our reading buddies from Mrs. Robison's fourth-grade class came to our room. My reading buddy is Michael Rimsky.

I like Michael. His smiles come fast, and his eyes sparkle behind his round glasses. I do not believe he ever combs his red hair. It always sticks out like he just climbed out of bed.

We sat down on the reading couch.

Lynette and her partner, Lissie Cook, sat right behind us on the floor. I peeked over the top of the couch. "Hi. What are you reading?"

Lissie held up a book. "Last week, Lynette said she wanted to learn more about Egypt. I found this book about it."

"It shows the Sphinx," Lynette said. "The Sphinx is that big stone statue in front of the pyramids. It has a lion body and a king head."

"I know that," I said.

"Oh, that's right. I forgot," Lynette said. "You know it all." She made a face. "You're Mrs. Arnold's special helper."

"I am," I said. "And I bet you're thinking THAT SPHINXS and you wish you were Mrs. Arnold's special helper. Get it? That STINKS, that SPHINXS?"

Lynette frowned. "Do you know what the Sphinx stands for?"

"I thought the Sphinx sat," I said, trying to make Lynette laugh. "So it *sits* for . . . a really, really, *really* long time."

"It *stands* for strength and wisdom," Lynette said with a la-de-da voice. "And that's not all—"

"And in case *you* didn't know," Lissie said, putting a hand on Lynette's shoulder, "wisdom is about using what you know to make good choices. Like being quiet now."

"A Sphinx can't be too strong or wise," I said, ignoring Lissie. "Part of its face fell off. So it doesn't *nose* much. But I have my whole face, so I *nose* a lot."

Lynette frowned. "Being smart-alecky isn't the same as being smart."

That comment chased away all the happy

in me. Forget about making Lynette laugh. If she didn't appreciate my smarty-smarts, I didn't need her.

"As soon as I prove I'm smarter than Sophie, I'll prove I'm smarter than you," I said. I grabbed the book Michael brought and shook it at her. "Now, excuse me while my reading buddy and I tackle this high-level book called—what is this book called, anyway?"

"*Froo Froo, the Happy-Yappy Poodle,*" Michael said.

What do you know! Lynette finally laughed.

I slouched into the couch cushions, my face burning. "At least it's not a book about ducks," I grumped.

Michael grinned. "If you want to look smart, try wearing glasses. People always tell me glasses make me look smarter."

"Ha, ha," I said, folding my arms across my chest. "Any other advice?"

Michael thought for a minute. "My dad says that reading books make you smarter."

"Somehow I don't think *Froo Froo, the Happy-Yappy Poodle* will help."

"Good point," Michael said. "So read a book written by someone really clever."

I scrunched up my face. "Does Dr. Seuss count? Because that man is a genius."

"Not unless you intend to beat this Sophie girl with a tongue-twisting poem." Michael opened up our book. "In the meantime, let's see what Froo Froo is up to."

"Wait!" I said, because something just popped BLAM into my head. "King Solomon."

"King who?"

"King Solomon. My grandpa says he was the smartest man who ever lived. He wrote a book called Proverbs."

"Your grandpa wrote a book called Proverbs?"

"No, King Solomon did."

"Like those proverbs you get in Chinese fortune cookies?"

"Yes," I said. "Only better. And without the cookie."

"Well, there you go then," Michael said. "Read Proverbs."

I frowned. "I can't. My Bible is at home. And I need more smartness before we go out for lunch recess."

"We'll have inside recess today. So you won't see Sophie," Michael said. "It's raining. Or didn't you notice?"

"I didn't notice."

Michael gave me one of his fast smiles. "In that case, I WILL give you some advice before I read this happy-yappy book to you. A smart person notices little details, like rain." He nodded toward Lynette. "And a smart person doesn't make enemies out of his best friends. But he does make friends out of his enemies."

"I see," I said. I pushed at his book. "And Froo-Froo?"

"Let's just say a smart person reads a story like Froo Froo for the brainless, mind-numbing fun of it."

6

King Solomon

While I waited for Mom to tuck me into bed that night, I took out my pocket Bible and found the book of Proverbs.

I like pocket Bibles. They are like regular Bibles only shrimpy sized, which makes them easier to handle. In some ways, pocket Bibles remind me of kids, because kids are like regular adults only shrimpy sized. Except that doesn't always make us easier to handle.

Anyway, guess what? King Solomon wrote a whole bunch of proverbs.

If I read them all, it would be like cracking open four huge bags stuffed with Chinese fortune cookies. Except eating so many cookies would give me a tummy ache. Plus I'd make a big mess. And I don't believe my dentist would be happy either.

"Meghan!" Mom yelled from downstairs. "Are you ready for bed?"

"No!" I yelled back. "I'm chewing on Chinese fortune cookies in my mind!"

"Really?" Mom hollered. "How many?"

"Lots and lots and lots and lots!" I hollered back.

I heard her footsteps clomping up the stairs. She opened my door and poked her head in. "It's getting late. Maybe you should nibble on just one cookie.'

I slapped my forehead. "Of course! I don't need all the verses. Just one."

"Verses? I thought you were talking about cookies."

"Exactly," I said. "Except these cookies are actually verses from Proverbs, which is in the Bible, which is God's Word and not Chinese or fortune or cookies at all."

"You lost me."

"I'm on my bed."

Mom sighed. "As long as I'm up here, would you like me to help you read your Bible?"

"Sure," I said. "One good verse will do. Can you find something about how to get smarter?"

"I'm not sure about getting smarter," Mom said, "but the Bible has a lot to say about gaining wisdom."

"Same thing," I said.

"Not really. Do you know what wisdom is?"

Thinking, I scrunched up my face. "Lissie Cook said wisdom is about using what you know to make good choices."

"Right. And I think smartness is simply knowing something."

"So . . . same thing," I said again.

This time Mom scrunched up her face. "Let's put it this way. Grandpa Wright knows all about rocks. That's smart. But when he built that retaining wall in the yard last summer, he chose what materials to use based on what he knew about rocks. That's wise."

"I remember," I said. "When we went to the store to get everything, I asked him why we had to buy rocks and why he didn't just take some rocks out of a field."

Mom smiled. "And how did he answer you?"

"He stopped by a field. We looked at the rocks there, and Grandpa asked questions. Is that rock hard or does it crumble? Is this one flat or round? I figured out not any old rock would do. We needed a certain type and size."

"Exactly."

"So maybe wisdom is more than just smart answers. Maybe it's about smart questions too."

"Maybe."

It was too much to think about. I decided to go back to my first question. "Can you give me a verse to help me or not?"

Mom flipped through the pages. "Here's half a verse. *With humility comes wisdom.*

Do you know what that means?"

"No," I said. "But don't tell me yet. Grandpa would want me to try and figure it out first."

"Suit yourself," Mom said. "I'll be back to say goodnight in ten minutes."

After she left, I thought about the verse. (And Grandpa, who rocks!) Forget wisdom. What on earth did *humility* mean? It sounded a little like another word I've heard— *humbleness*. They were probably the same thing. And they probably had something to do with bumblebees. *Humble. Bumble.*

I was full of bumblebee-ness. Buzz-buzz. That's me. Which meant I probably already had all the smarts I needed to face Sophie again. She might surprise me with a spelling or math or history test, but I could test her right back.

Not that I actually knew any tests. Mom says I know how to test her patience, but I believe that's something else entirely.

I could test Sophie about rocks. Plus I knew all sorts of interesting things I bet she didn't know. Like the dot over the letter *i* is called a *tittle*. Lynette told me that once when she was in a show-off mood.

Plus I probably could stump Sophie with this interesting fact, something I figured out on my own. If it's a really small letter *i*, you call the dot a *little tittle*.

And if it's really, really small, it's an *itsy-bitsy little tittle*.

Any smaller, and it's a *teensy-weensy, itsy-bitsy, little tittle*.

But what if testing Sophie about rocks and tittles didn't work? I'd need to do something with *humility*. Hmm. *Humbleness* rhymed with *crumble-ness*, *fumble-ness*, *grumble-ness*, *mumble-ness*, *stumble-ness*, and *tumble-ness*. Maybe I could beat Sophie with a tongue-twisting poem after all!

Mom came back. "I'll bet I'm the smartest girl in first grade," I said.

She laughed. "Maybe. But don't brag too much, or you might have to swallow your pride."

I didn't plan on swallowing anything. "Am I like a bumblebee?"

Puffing her cheeks, Mom studied me. "Always busy and buzzy. You bet!"

HA! Sophie didn't stand a chance.

With all the humble-bumble, little-tittle thoughts going through my head, I fell asleep with a smile on my face.

I do not believe I would have slept so well if I had known what Sophie had planned.

7

Ka-Ching!

"We keep it simple," Sophie said the next day on the playground. "Each person scores a point when she outsmarts the other person on any task or test or anything else."

"OK," I said. "What should we do first?"

Sophie gave me a sugary smile. "*Ka-ching*. One point for me." She licked her finger and made an invisible mark in the air.

"What?" I cried.

Sophie faced the kids there to watch the contest. "I just outsmarted Meghan into agreeing to my rules."

"You didn't outsmart me," I said. "I was just being friendly."

"I think she outsmarted you," Carly said. "I say the point stands."

I ground my teeth. So this is how it would work. Carly would back up everything Sophie said, whether it was fair or not.

"I won the first point, so I choose the first test," Sophie said.

A dozen sets of eyes turned toward me. "Fine," I growled.

"*Ka-ching*," Sophie said. "Two points for me. I just outsmarted you into letting me go first."

"So I'm a pushover. That doesn't mean

you're smarter than me," I said.

"I say the point stands!" yelled Carly.

"Yay!" other kids cheered.

"The first test is a memory test," Sophie said. "We'll each look at a picture for one minute. Then we'll write down what we remember seeing in the picture. The one who remembers the most wins. I brought paper and pencils."

I took a quick peek at Carly and spotted the corner of a postcard sticking out of her pocket. I bet Sophie would ask if anyone had a picture, and Carly would just happen to have one—one Sophie had memorized already.

"Why use a picture?" I said quickly. "We're already standing here with our backs to most of the playground. I say we turn around and look, then turn back and write.

That seems like the easiest way to do it."

"Good idea," Ryan said. Several other kids nodded in agreement. Carly hesitated, but finally she nodded too.

Sophie's face turned red. I knew I had her. I smiled. "*Ka-ching*."

When the test ended, Sophie had listed eleven things—the swing set, two teachers, basketballs, basketball hoops, monkey bars, slide, sand, tree, grass, a yellow bus, and kids playing.

I had listed all those things plus one more—a jump rope. I'd seen Lynette take a jump rope out to recess. I knew she'd go by the swing set, where we always jump.

Except she went without me today. Again.

"*Ka-ching*!" Kayla yelled. "The score is tied."

Sophie scowled. "The next test is—"

"Mine to choose," I interrupted.

"I changed my mind about that. This contest was my idea," Sophie said, "so I get to pick the activities."

Ryan stepped between us. "The only way to keep the contest fair is to take turns." The kids around us seemed to agree, so Sophie did too.

I thought for a minute. I decided not to ask a tricky question, like my tittle one. Sophie was so sneaky, that could turn out bad for me. Maybe I could beat her with poetry after all. "You have to make up a limerick using the other person's name."

"What's a limerick?" Sophie said.

"*KA-CHING!*" Kayla yelled. "If Meghan has to explain it, that's got to be worth a point."

I grinned. "A limerick is a rhyming poem. You can follow my example—

There once was a baker named Sophie,

Who wanted to win a big trophy.

She mixed eggs and flour,

And cooked for an hour,

But came home with just a bread loafy."

"No way," Sophie said. "I'm not making up a limerick. That proves you're silly, not smart. Besides, nothing rhymes with Meghan."

"Begging does. And legging. Kind of."

"Fine," Sophie snapped. "But *loafy* isn't a real word."

"That's what makes it so clever," I said.

"*Ka-ching* for me anyway, since your test is undoable."

"I'll think of something else then."

"No. My turn," Sophie said. "You lost

your turn. Now I've got a riddle for you. What animal always needs cash and why?"

"Ha!" Ryan said. "Meghan is GREAT at riddles."

I swallowed hard. Ryan thought I was great because I answered all of his rock riddles. He didn't realize I'm not so good with riddles when I don't already know the answers.

8

Buzz Buzz

While everyone stared and waited for me to answer, I chewed my lip.

Think. Think. What animal always needs cash and why? A deer? A male deer is a buck—and a buck is a dollar—and a female deer a doe—or dough, as in money. But the answer couldn't be deer. Deer don't need cash. They'd always have a buck and more doe.

A sand dollar? No, that wouldn't work

for the same reason as the deer.

A skunk? A skunk smells, or makes scents. *Scents* sounds like *cents*, and cents is money. So a skunk doesn't need cash because it has scents. Cents. Whatever.

I wished Lynette were here to give me ideas. She always thinks things through. But instead of helping me, she was over by the swing set jumping rope. In fact, she hadn't talked to me all day.

Was she avoiding me?

Then I remembered how her face looked red and angry when everyone said, "Meghan Rose knows it all" and *oohed* and *ahhed* over me. And the face she made during reading buddies when she reminded me that I was Mrs. Arnold's special helper.

And the way I acted both times.

A wave of *oh-no* hit me.

Sophie interrupted my thoughts. "Hurry up! Or else it's *ka-ching* for me, and you lose."

No more time to worry about Lynette. Instead, I squeezed my eyes shut. Even when you're Einstein smart, in situations like this, it's best to pray.

"Dear God," I whispered in my head. "I need to know what to do. Help!"

Solomon's proverb popped into my head. *With humility comes wisdom.*

So with humilty comes the ability to use what you know to make good choices. What did I know about being humble I could use?

Humble. Bumble.

"Buzz buzz," I said. Nothing happened.

Sophie scrunched up her nose. "What are you doing?"

Ignoring her, I stuck my arms out like wings. "Buzzzzzzz. Buzzzzzz." I ran around in a circle. "Buzzzzzz. Buzzzzzz. Buzzzzzz."

"What is she doing?" Ryan whispered.

"I don't know," Kayla squealed. "But I'm going to do it too!"

First Kayla, then Ryan, then Abigail, then Adam, and then the rest joined me. We zipped around in a line. We raced down to the monkey bars and back again, buzzing and laughing all the way.

"Is that your answer?" Sophie screamed, stomping her foot. We skidded to a stop. "Is that your silly, ridiculous answer? A bee?"

I took a big breath.

I needed . . . I needed . . . Then BLAM, what Kayla said I needed yesterday popped into my head.

Add more ducks.

"DUCKS!" I cried. "The answer is ducks."

Sophie looked like she might spit.

"Is that right?" Carly asked. Sophie glared at her. Carly quickly added, "Not that I think it's a good answer or anything."

Sophie huffed. "It's right. Except Meghan forgot to say why. So *ka-ching* for me. I win."

"Wait," I said. "I wasn't done. The answer is ducks because ducks have bills. That's why they need cash. To pay their bills."

"Finally," Kayla said. "It's about time someone paid attention to ducks."

"*Ka-ching*," Ryan said. "We're tied again."

"Hang on," I said. "I'm still not done."

Sophie sneered. "I suppose you have a

riddle for me? We could go on like this all day."

"We could go on like this all year," I said. "But I've got a way to end this contest."

"You can end it," Sophie said, "by giving up and admitting that I'm smarter than you."

I held up a finger. "Yes, but I'm not going to do that because I don't need to be smarter. I need wisdom."

I looked over to where Lynette sat on the playground. "And in this case that means I need more ducks."

Sophie snarled, ignoring me. "OR you could suffer a humiliating defeat, and THEN give up and admit I'm smarter than you."

I paused. "Humiliating? I don't suppose that has anything to do with bumblebees, does it?"

Sophie snorted. "No. *Humiliate*. As in me putting you to shame."

I tapped my chin. "And I don't suppose that has anything to do with humility?"

"I think those two words mean different things," Carly said, "*Humiliate* means to embarrass. *Humility* means you don't brag or go around acting all important. Or you don't expect special treatment."

Sophie glared at her.

Carly quickly added, "Not that I know anyone like that."

"I see," I said.

Then BLAM, something my mom had said popped into my head. "So humility is like swallowing your pride."

"I swallowed my gum once," Ryan said. "It was an accident."

"I swallowed a bug once," Kayla said.

"But I did it on purpose. I thought it was a raisin."

"Enough!" Sophie growled. "Do you give up or what?"

9

Adding More Ducks

"Don't give up," Ryan said, nudging me with his elbow. "Recess isn't over yet, and I want to hear your idea about more ducks."

"Me too!" Kayla said. A whole chorus of me-toos filled the air. I even heard Carly.

I looked at Sophie. "If this doesn't work out, you can humiliate me PLUS I'll give up."

Sophie's eyes seemed to flare up like a match. "Promise?"

"Promise."

"Deal," she said. "What's your idea?"

"There's something I have to do first."

"We haven't got all day."

"I only need a few minutes," I said. "I'll be right back." And I ran off.

I found Lynette sitting on a bench. Her jump rope lay on the ground nearby. She had a sour-pickle look on her face.

"What do you want?" Lynette grumped as I plopped down next to her.

I took a big breath. And I did something hard to do. I swallowed my pride.

"I want to say I'm sorry."

Swallowing my pride wasn't like swallowing a mouthful of chips, like Kayla did at lunch on Monday. It was more like trying to swallow an entire water buffalo in one bite—a water buffalo that went on an eating spree and popped the button on its pants.

(Not that I've ever tried swallowing a water buffalo before, and not that they wear pants, but you know what I mean. It wasn't easy.)

Lynette blinked at me. Her lip trembled. "Sorry for what?"

I sighed. "It's a long story and I only have a few minutes to talk before I go back and either beat Sophie or give up."

Lynette cleared her throat. "Give up? I thought you knew everything."

"I thought I knew everything too," I said. I slouched. "But there was something important I didn't know. I didn't know about humility and wisdom."

"Let me guess," Lynette said. "You thought being humble had something to do with bees."

"How did you know?"

Lynette grinned. "You buzzed past me on the playground."

We laughed. Then I said, "I know why you've been staying away from me. I've been bragging about how smart I am."

"Yeah," Lynette said. "And you kept bragging about being Mrs. Arnold's special helper."

"That too."

"And you hurt my feelings by making fun of the Sphinx."

"I know," I said. I kept going. "You said the Sphinx stands for wisdom?"

"Yes," Lynette said.

"I found a verse in the Bible that says, 'With humility comes wisdom.' But I didn't REALLY understand what wisdom is until

I figured out humility. Then I also figured out I haven't been treating you nicely. And now I see what a silly goose I've been."

"Silly goose? I thought you were a bumblebee."

"Ha, ha," I said. "The truth is, I know a lot, but I don't know it all."

Lynette looked at the ground. Then she must have swallowed her pride too, because she said, "Me neither."

"But I know a lot more when I'm with you," I said. "We make a rock-solid team. The smartest and the wisest thing I can do right now is say I'm sorry. Will you forgive me?"

Lynette nodded. She looked like she might cry.

"Good," I said. "Because I'm not done. I also realized Kayla was right. We need more ducks."

Lynette frowned. "More ducks?"

I pointed back to where Sophie and the others were waiting. "Yes. I need you to come back there with me. One more duck ought to do it."

"I don't understand."

I grabbed her arm and dragged her after me.

"You will when we get there," I said. "If we're lucky, we still have time to pull this thing off!"

10

Meghan Rose Knows It All

"It took you long enough," Sophie snapped when I got back. "And how nice. You brought along my second-least-favorite person. I wondered where she was hiding."

Lynette's face turned red. She opened her mouth to say something, but I stopped her. "I answered your riddle, Sophie. It's my turn."

I faced all the kids. "For this contest, I need everyone except me to sit in a circle."

Kids pushed for spots on the grass. Only Sophie didn't move. "Remember . . . when this flops, you give up."

I shrugged. "*If* this flops, I will. Now hurry up. We haven't got all day."

Sophie folded her arms across her chest. "Is this another Concentration game?"

"No."

"A riddle using people?"

"No."

"A math puzzle?"

"You *really* don't know me very well, do you?"

Sophie glared at me.

"Never mind," I said, waving my hand. "Sit down or I'll win automatically."

Sophie sat.

I clapped my hands for attention.

"First, I have something important to tell

you. Sophie is smart."

"Ha!" Sophie jumped to her feet. "I told you!"

"But," I went on, "I'm smart too. Does it matter who is smartest?"

"YES!" Sophie said.

I put my hands on my hips. "Yay for you. Now can I finish?"

Sophie stuck out her lip but kept quiet.

I went on. "Smart isn't enough for me anymore. Because I figured out that there's a difference between smartness and wisdom. Smartness is stuff you know in your head, up here." I tapped my forehead. "Wisdom is using what you know in your head to make good choices here." I tapped my heart.

"I don't get it," Kayla said.

BLAM! Just then I had an idea that somehow I knew was very wise indeed.

"Mrs. Arnold showed us a pumice rock. It looks like a sponge. My grandpa says it's *abrasive*. That's a fancy word for *rough*. In fact, some people use pumice to scrape off old dry skin.

"If *smart* was a rock, it would be like pumice. Being smart is good, but if you don't use smartness right, it can rub people the wrong way.

"Wisdom is more like a geode. It can seem bumble-humble, simple-and-plain on the outside, but inside it holds a sparkly treasure. And you don't rub people with it . . . you very gently open it up and share it with them."

"What on earth?" Sophie roared. "You've hit rock bottom."

I laughed. "Earth. Rock bottom. Good joke!"

"I don't get it," Kayla said.

"It wasn't a joke," Sophie said.

"So I shouldn't laugh?" Kayla asked.

"No!" Sophie said.

"Can I laugh anyway?" Kayla said. "I like laughing."

"NO!" Sophie snapped. "NO, NO, NO!"

"Never mind, Kayla," I said. "Right now, wisdom is telling me it's time for fun. So . . ." I started walking around the circle. "Duck, duck, duck—"

"WHAT?" Sophie sputtered. She jumped in front of me. "I'm not playing Duck, Duck, Goose." She poked her finger at my chest. "Beat me fair and square with your brain or GIVE UP and ADMIT I'm the smartest."

Then without a word, Lynette popped up from her spot and stood quietly beside me.

Wowie.

So I didn't yell back at Sophie. Instead, I used a calm, soft voice and said, "Sophie, do you know what a *tittle* is?"

Sophie's eyes went wide. "A—a little?"

"No, a *tittle*. Do you know what a *tittle* is?"

"I've never heard of it," Sophie whispered back. "You're making it up."

"No, she's not," Lynette said. "I know what a tittle is."

I smiled at Lynette. "Me too. Sophie?"

Sophie clenched her fists, but she didn't say anything. Finally she sat back down like a stiff piece of cardboard. I gave her a thumbs up and started walking again. "Duck, duck, duck, GOOSE!"

Sophie steamed like an igneous lava rock the whole game. On Kayla's turn, Kayla goosed Sophie, but Sophie folded her arms and *harrumphed.*

Kayla goosed her twice more and then gave up. She called her a chicken instead and goosed Carly.

When Carly jumped up, Kalya squealed and raced around the circle with her arms flapping all over the place like wet noodles.

She ran past her stop point three times, squealing all the way.

And she changed direction twice, making Carly fall each time. And leapfrogged into

the wrong spot, knocking over three boys. She squealed again when she realized her mistake, and then she scampered across the middle of the circle like a crab, squealing all the way.

Carly collapsed onto the ground in a fit of laughter.

I laughed so hard I thought my tummy might burst open.

We all did. And finally . . . *even Sophie* started laughing. Then she right away hid her face behind her hair. But she still couldn't help peeking.

Eventually she gave up trying to be tough and went flat out *ha-ha-ha*. Which, I believe, was the smart thing to do.

We had a blast—me and my friends and Sophie and her friends. It was especially *gneiss* to have Lynette with me.

I'm glad things turned out OK. Plus I learned something. Like I guess wisdom isn't so much about what you know but about what you're willing to learn. And for that, you need a lot of buzz-buzz humility and a water-buffalo sized fork. And maybe even a few more ducks.

Chatter Matters

1. Read the story of the wise builder and the foolish builder found in Matthew 7:24–27. What is the difference between how the two men built their houses? What actions can we take each day to "build our houses" (or live) on the solid rock (Jesus)?

2. In your own words, tell what you think the word *humility* means. What kind of trouble do you think bragging causes? What can you do to stay humble?

3. What is the best piece of advice or wisdom you have ever heard? How did it help you?

4. Read Proverbs 12:15 and Proverbs 19:20. Where can you find advice? How can you tell if advice your friend gives you is worth following or not? If you could give advice to Meghan Rose, what would you tell her? If you could give advice to Sophie, what would you tell her?

5. Tell about a time when you had to apologize to someone. How did you feel afterward? Were you glad you did it? Why or why not? How do you react when a friend tells you she is sorry? See what the Bible says about forgiveness in Luke 17:3.

Blam! – Great Activity Ideas

1. Play Duck, Duck, Goose with your friends. Invite children in your neighborhood or school that you don't know well to join you.

2. Collect a dozen or so rocks from outside. Study them carefully and then sort them by color, shape, size, or other attributes you can think of. For an extra challenge, make your rock sorting into a game!

Make two circles out of yarn. Pick a sorting rule. Put rocks that fit your rule into one yarn circle and rocks that don't fit your rule into the other circle. Ask a friend to guess your rule. Here's the catch: before guessing, she must correctly sort three rocks.

3. Make a pet rock. You will need a fist-sized rock, permanent markers, wiggle eyes, and any other craft supply you want to use to decorate. A hot-glue gun works well to attach objects, but be sure to ask a handy adult to help you use it.

4. Make rock candy. (This can take up to a week.) You need 1 cup of water, 2 cups of granulated sugar, ¼–½ teaspoon of flavoring (like unsweetened grape or cherry drink mix), food coloring, a pot, a clean glass jar, a pencil, a paper clip, and yarn.

First, cut the yarn a little longer than the jar is tall. Tie one end of the yarn to the middle of the pencil. Tie the other end around a paper clip. Place the pencil across the top of the jar and wind it until the thread is hanging about one inch from the bottom. Next, wet the yarn and then roll it in the sugar. (This gives the rock crystals something to grow on.) Set the yarn aside.

Next, prepare a sugar mixture. (You might want a handy adult to help you with this part.) Boil the water in the pan. Add the sugar, ½ cup at a time, stirring after each addition. (The more sugar you add, the longer it will take to dissolve.) Keep stirring and boiling the mixture until all the sugar has been added and dissolved.

Remove the pan from the heat. Add two or three drops of food coloring and ½ teaspoon of flavor. Stir well. Let the sugar mixture cool for ten minutes. (This is the hard part . . . you'll have to WAIT! Argh!)

Pour the sugar mixture into the jar. Now

set the pencil with the sugared yarn across the top of the jar. Loosely cover the top with plastic wrap or a paper towel. Put the jar in a dark, cool place (where you can watch it but won't be tempted to move it around).

Sugar crystals should start forming within two to four hours. (If nothing happens after a day, boil the sugar mixture again, dissolve another cup of sugar into it, and then pour it back into the jar.) Now watch and wait! When the rock candy reaches the size you want, take it out, let it dry for a few minutes, and then eat it up. Yum, yum!

5. Create an edible model of sedimentary rock. (Just so you know, sedimentary rocks are rocks that form when layers of sand, pebbles, clay, plants, bones, and mud are

piled on top of each other. The layers get squished down—like a dog pile—and eventually get hard. In rocks, the layers look like stripes.) You will need bread, cookie (or graham cracker) crumbs, red or purple jelly, raisins (or chocolate chips), peanut butter (unless you are allergic to peanuts), marshmallow cream spread (but only if you like marshmallows), a plastic knife, and a plate.

First, draw freely on your imagination. Pretend each food item is a layer in your sedimentary rock. The bread stands for sand. Peanut butter stands for mud, and raisins or chocolate chips for rocks. The jelly and cookie crumbs are for old decaying plants and bones, and the marshmallow cream for clay.

Starting with the bread as the bottom layer, create your sedimentary rock model. Add as many layers as you want. You can even put extra layers of bread between the spreads. Then, TADA! You have a science rock model you can eat. (If you'd like to see what happens when the earth moves, bend your sandwich and watch what happens to the layers. Just don't bend it too far or . . . EARTHQUAKE!)

For families:
Brow, Kussman, Hoskins, and Brown—LZS

For Shana—SC

Lori Z. Scott graduated from Wheaton College
eons ago. She is a second-grade teacher, a wife, the
mother of two busy teenagers, and a writer. Lori has
published over one hundred articles, short stories,
devotions, puzzles, and poems and has contributed
to over a dozen books.

In her spare time Lori loves doodling, reading the
Sunday comics, and making up lame jokes.

You can find out more about Lori and her books
at www.MeghanRoseSeries.com.

Stacy Curtis is a cartoonist, illustrator,
printmaker, and twin who's illustrated over twenty
children's books, including a *New York Times* best
seller. He and his wife, Jann, live in Oak Lawn,
Illinois, and happily share their home with their dog,
Derby.

Meghan Rose
is bouncing your way!

978-0-7847-2103-2

978-0-7847-2105-6

Meghan Rose On Stage!
Lori Z. Scott
Illustrated by Stacy Curtis

Meghan Rose Has Ants in Her Pants
Lori Z. Scott
Illustrated by Stacy Curtis

Meghan Rose All Dressed Up
Lori Z. Scott
Illustrated by Stacy Curtis

Meghan Rose Has a Secret
Lori Z. Scott
Illustrated by Stacy Curtis

978-0-7847-2106-3

978-0-7847-2107-0

978-0-7847-2930-4

Meghan Rose Takes the Cake
Lori Z. Scott
Illustrated by Stacy Curtis

Meghan Rose Knows It All
Lori Z. Scott
Illustrated by Stacy Curtis

978-0-7847-2931-1

978-0-7847-2933-5

Meghan Rose Is Out of This World
Lori Z. Scott
Illustrated by Stacy Curtis

Meghan Rose Is Tickled Pinkish Orange
Lori Z. Scott
Illustrated by Stacy Curtis

978-0-7847-2932-8

**To order these titles
visit www.standardpub.com
or call 1-800-543-1353.**